This English edition published in 2017 under license from big & SMALL
by Eerdmans Books for Young Readers,
an imprint of Wm. B. Eerdmans Publishing Co.
2140 Oak Industrial Dr. NE, Grand Rapids, Michigan 49505
www.eerdmans.com/youngreaders

Original Korean text by Jeong-hee Nam • Illustrations by Lucia Sforza • Edited by Joy Cowley
Original Korean edition © Yeowon Media Co., Ltd. • English edition © big & SMALL 2014

17 18 19 20 21 22 23   9 8 7 6 5 4 3 2 1

Manufactured at Tien Wah Press in Malaysia

Names: Nam, Jeong-hee, 1971- author. | Sforza, Lucia, illustrator. | Cowley,
    Joy, editor.
Title: Lion, king, and coin / written by Jeong-hee Nam ; illustrated by Lucia
    Sforza ; edited by Joy Cowley.
Description: Grand Rapids, MI : Eerdmans Books for Young Readers, 2017. |
    Series: Trade winds | Summary: "When trading goods at the market becomes
    increasingly difficult, Laos's family is commissioned to make the world's
    first coin"— Provided by publisher.
Identifiers: LCCN 2016024378 | ISBN 9780802854759
Subjects: | CYAC: Coins — History — Fiction.
Classification: LCC PZ7.1.N355 Li 2017 | DDC [Fic] — dc23 LC record available at
    https://lccn.loc.gov/2016024378

Display type set in Brubeck AH
Text type set in Garamond

Lion, King, and Coin

Written by **Jeong-hee Nam**
Illustrated by **Lucia Sforza**
Edited by **Joy Cowley**

Eerdmans Books for Young Readers

Grand Rapids, Michigan

In our village, the Pactolus River is also called the "golden river" because it has real gold in its sandy banks. Coins made from this gold are the pride of our great village, Sardis.

Do you want to know how these coins were invented? Well, here is my story.

My name is Laos, and I live with my parents, uncle, and grandfather.

Grandpa and Dad work at a blacksmith's forge. They melt gold dust and shape it into ornaments so beautiful that the king has awarded them for their skill.

My uncle sells gold at the market. I help him at his stall or go to the Pactolus River to look for gold dust.

I am good at finding gold dust in the sand.
I stick a plate deep in the river,
take it out, and shake it in water.

The light sand washes off,
  and the heavy gold is left.

One day I asked Grandpa a question:
"Why is there gold in the Pactolus River?"

Grandpa told me the myth about King Midas.

King Midas wanted to be the richest man in the world.

One day, someone wandered into King Midas's garden
and got lost. It was Silenus, the foster father
of Dionysus, who was the god of wine and fertility.
King Midas treated Silenus with great kindness.

Silenus praised King Midas to Dionysus,
who visited the king to express his gratitude.
"I will grant you one wish," said Dionysus.

King Midas replied, "Whatever I touch,
let it be turned into gold."

Dionysus was not happy with the wish, but he granted it,
and that is how King Midas got his "golden touch."

When King Midas sat down to dinner,
the bread he picked up turned to gold.
His daughter Aurelia began to cry
when she saw that her father couldn't eat.
King Midas reached out his hand
to comfort Aurelia, but she too turned to gold.

Sobbing, King Midas ran to Dionysus
and begged him to take away the wish.
Dionysus said, "Go to the Pactolus River
and wash your body of greed."

The king obeyed, and as he washed himself,
his golden touch disappeared and his
daughter was brought back to him.

Since that day, the sand in the Pactolus River
has been filled with gold.

Some time later, I went to the market to help Uncle.
There were many stalls at the market, with people
selling everything from fruit and jewelry to dyed
wool and pots of perfumed cream.

My uncle's stall was crowded
with people trading goods for gold.
There was a lot of shouting.

"Please trade these apples for gold."

"Our honey is just as valuable as gold."

"How do I know if this gold is good?"

"How can I trust your word?"

"Hurry up, will you?"

People brought many things,
including live animals,
to trade for pieces of gold.
Poor Uncle was very busy.

A shepherd said loudly to Uncle,
"I want only one piece of fruit, so how can
I trade a whole sheep for it?"

My uncle complained, "Gold is easy.
You can weigh and cut gold,
but you can't cut an animal in half.
The last time I traded gold for a cow,
the cow ran away."

The next day, Uncle went to the market
and spoke to all the stall owners.

"We need something that can replace
the value of the things we sell.
It needs to be light and easy to carry.
It must be something that will not rot.
Maybe it should be made of gold or silver."

Everyone nodded in agreement.

People wondered who would decide its value.
It needed to be someone everybody respected,
someone everybody would listen to.

I suggested, "Why don't we ask the king?"

Everyone thought that was a good plan.
So my uncle wrote down all these ideas
and took them to the high priest.

When the king heard about this,
he had a piece of gold engraved
to show its value. He called this a coin.
Then the king issued a decree
that coins be used for everything
that was bought or sold.

The king instructed Dad and Grandpa
to make coins at their forge.
When Grandpa explained to me
what they were doing, I asked him,
"Why are you printing the head of a lion?"

"The lion is the king of the jungle,"
he said. "The lion represents the king.
The pictures engraved on these coins
show the king's power and authority."

It was hard work to make a coin. First the gold had to be weighed, then melted. The melted gold was poured into a circular frame with the lion's head engraved on the bottom. Finally, using a hammer, the gold was hit hard to give the coin its shape.

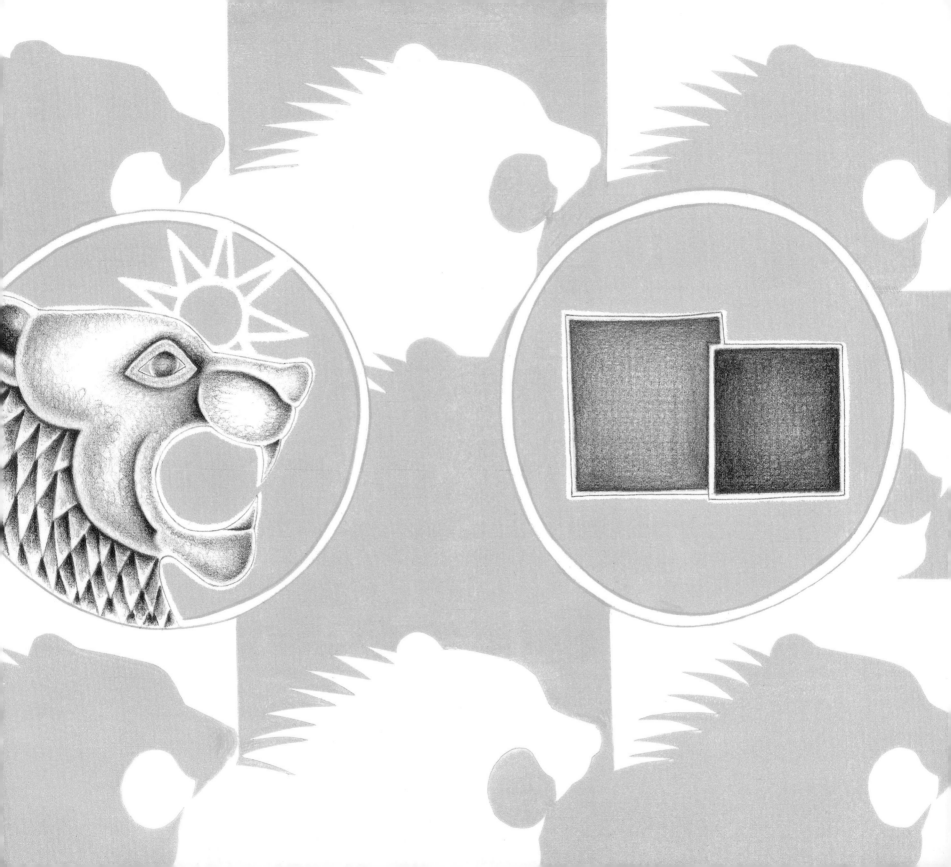

When the coin was finished,
it was called an electrum coin.
On the front of the coin was the lion's head,
and on the back of the coin were the imprints
from the hammer blows.

My uncle's stall is peaceful now.
All he does is sell pieces of gold
and accept coins in exchange.
The shepherd can now sell his sheep
and buy what he needs
with the coins he receives.

Everyone is happy that they can buy and sell easily. All they need are coins to exchange for their items.

The Invention of the Coin

Even before the coin was created, Lydia was home to many bustling marketplaces. Merchants traded food and livestock, as well as more luxurious items, like perfume and fine jewelry. With so many different items being offered, the Lydians needed to make sure that everyone in the crowded marketplaces received a fair trade. They achieved this with the invention of currency.

The first known coin was created during the reign of King Alyattes sometime between the seventh and sixth century BCE. Made of electrum — a naturally occurring mixture of gold and silver — the coins were lightweight, portable, and durable. Different denominations of coins were created, all based on a standard unit of measurement, thus establishing a fluid form of currency.

Coins were precisely weighed and molded, and then stamped. Distinctive stamps on the coins made counterfeiting difficult, which helped merchants to ensure an honest trade. The stamp also provided a symbolic reminder of the king's power. The lion, king of the jungle, was featured on Lydian coins to represent the king's authority.

With the invention of money, anything could be bought or sold at any time. Because everyone in the marketplace used the same form of currency, consistent prices could be established based on supply and demand. This allowed the region's economy to grow and flourish. It wasn't long before other parts of the world created their own coinage, which led to a robust network of commerce.

The Geography of Sardis

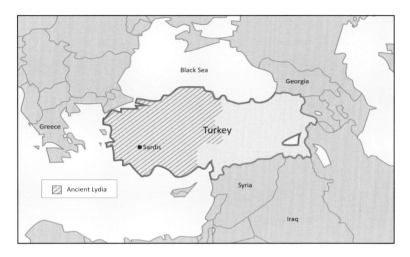

The map above shows Sardis and ancient Lydia in the context of modern-day borders.

Lion, King, and Coin is set in the ancient kingdom of Lydia, which was located in Asia Minor. The climate there was temperate, and the land was fertile and rich in minerals. Sardis — Lydia's capital — was located near the Pactolus River, where the legendary King Midas washed away his golden touch. However, the gold dust in the Pactolus came not from Midas, but from the nearby mountains as the river ran downstream. Regardless of its origin, the gold dust that washed up on the banks of the Pactolus made the creation of coined money possible and ultimately changed the world of commerce.

Key Terms and Concepts

Currency is a widely accepted form of payment. As an established form of compensation that was convenient for everyone, currency simplified the process of buying and selling, thus revolutionizing the region's economy.

A **barter** is an exchange in which an item is traded for another item. With the invention of currency, bartering became unnecessary.

Although irregular in size and shape, early electrum coins were minted according to a strict weight standard, called **stater**. With a standard unit in place, different **denominations**, or values, could be created. The Lydian electrum coin, for example, was one-third stater.

Coins were manufactured through a process called **minting**, which ensured that the metals were accurately measured and properly stamped. Modern institutions responsible for the production of coins and other money are called **mints**.

Precursors to Money

Before the invention of money, people relied on bartering to acquire the goods and services they needed. But the system of bartering came with complications and limitations. It was difficult to find an equal exchange for the fair value of merchandise. Farmers could not barter for crops that had not yet been harvested. Many common items used for bartering, like blocks of metal or bags of grain, were heavy and difficult to carry to and from the market. Because of this, merchants started using small tokens for trading, since they could easily be transported and counted. Such tokens included:

feathers   cowrie shells

beads   whale teeth

While these items made trading easier, there was still a need to establish a consistent system for buying and selling goods according to their value. With the Lydian coin, people could ensure that exchanges were equal and fair, and they could more easily accumulate wealth. The invention of currency allowed the trading system to develop and expand, eventually leading to the global economy we have today.

For Example

In the barter system, if a merchant had a clay pot but wanted a bushel of apples, he would have had to find a farmer willing to exchange his apples for a pot. Once money was invented, the merchant could sell his clay pot at a good price and use the money to buy the apples.

A Timeline of Events

(Due to the limited information we have about these ancient times, some dates are approximations.)

9,000-8,000 BCE
Obsidian, a kind of volcanic glass valued during the Stone Age for its use in making tools, is traded throughout the Mediterranean.

9000 BCE
Cattle and grain begin to be used as a standard form of barter.

1200 BCE
In China, people begin to use cowrie shells as currency.

1000 BCE
Tools such as knives and spades are used as currency in China. Eventually, the sharp edges of these metal tools are rounded to allow for easier transport.

600 BCE
The world's first coin — the Lydian Lion — is developed in Sardis. Electrum coins soon spread throughout Greece and Asia Minor.

400s BCE
A coin called the Athenian Owl is minted in enormous quantities in Greece. It becomes the first coin widely used in international trade.

269 BCE
Rome establishes a mint at the Temple of Juno Moneta, goddess of funds. The word *money* is derived from her name.

118 BCE
Leather money is used in China in the form of strips of white deerskin with colorful borders. This became a precursor to banknotes.

1120s CE
The Song Dynasty in China starts producing the world's first government-issued paper money.